FRISKY CONNECTIONS

A Frisky Bean Prequel Novelette

MICHELLE MARS

Copyright © 2019 by Michelle Mars

All rights reserved.

No part of this book may be reproduced in any form or by any electronic or mechanical means, including information storage and retrieval systems, without written permission from the author, except for the use of brief quotations in a book review.

This is a work of fiction. Names, characters, places, and incidents, are products of the author's imagination or are used fictitiously. Any resemblance to actual events, locales, organizations, or persons, living or dead, is entirely coincidental.

A version of this story can be found in the anthology Eight Kisses.

Cover design by Leni Kauffman

❦ Created with Vellum

I would like to dedicate this book to all the Jewish romance writers out here delivering the representation I searched for when I was growing up. And to the readers who pick up a book with Jewish characters either because they see themselves in the stories or because they know that love is universal and are open to sharing in a story different than their own.

With both love and latkes, it's better when sticking together. <3

CHAPTER ONE

"Really. It's fine, honey. You couldn't have predicted a bird bombing as soon as you stepped out of the house. I'd turn right around and need a shower too." Shira Abramson spoke into her phone, tempering her disappointment and comforting her friend Keren Sabinski once again.

As her friend apologized for the hundredth time, she returned, "I *know* you'd come if you could. We both knew this was going to have to be a quick get together as it was."

Keren finally said, "I know. I know. It's just that I was so fucking excited to see you. It's been too long. I feel sooo bad. And instead of girl chat, I get to remove bird shit from my hair. Ew."

"I think I come out just fine compared to you, so don't worry even for a second. I'll just grab a quick coffee and get some work done. No biggie."

"Actually, if you still plan to grab a coffee, might I suggest you try out my company's new app?"

"Which app?"

"Immedia-Date."

"The dating app you described to me last month?"

"Yep. The very one. It's just come out this week and we've already had a ton of people sign up. Give it a try. Maybe you'll meet Mr. Right today and shitting birds will have a silver lining. It would be good for your blog *and* you can provide me with feedback."

"You're such a yenta."

"I'll wear that matchmaking badge with pride, thank you very much. Yenta heart. Business brain. Now give it a go, and I'm going to wash my hair a million times over and then head to my meeting."

"Fine. If I end up dead in a ditch somewhere, I'll know who to blame." Shira grumbled.

"Enjoy. Avoid the ditch. Text your bitch. That sounded a lot better in my head than out loud. You know what I mean, though. Text me when you're done. Bye."

With that, the line went dead.

What had she just agreed to? Shira opened up the app store and searched for Immedia-Date. She located it and had it downloaded quickly. She was impressed right away with the ease of setting it up. The streamlined process was a snap. Answer a few simple questions and it created a basic profile with what you were looking for. Tall, dark, Jewish a bonus, and handsome a desire. The app prompted that all she needed to do now, was turn her profile to 'currently available' and it would search her vicinity for any available matches interested in a short pop-up date. So she did just that. Easy peasy.

Her phone dinged almost right away, making her jump. Someone was available and interested in meeting up with her. *Well, that was fast.*

She opened the app back up, clicked on the profile of the interested party, and had to blink a few times. This had to be a scam. No one joined a dating app and got one of the hottest guys she'd ever seen in the first couple of minutes. She bet it was someone catfishing with a fake picture, but that could be resolved quickly when they met, so she clicked "Interested." The app took a minute to search the area between them for a highly rated coffee shop or café within a short distance.

Her phone dinged again with the address to the shop. Shira figured she would at least discover a new place to get her caffeine fix out of this ill-advised adventure into modern dating. Coffee was life, after all. She pulled out of the parking lot where she had meant to meet Keren and headed to her Immedia-Date with some trepidation laced with excitement.

She arrived a few minutes later at her destination and was intrigued by the place right away. She checked out the map on the app and her date was still a few minutes away, so she decided to investigate the place on her own. The front window boasted a sign that read:

Welcome to The Frisky Bean
Coffee to Wake You Up
Pastries to Turn You On

Shira was now more than intrigued. What kind of crazy coffee place was this? And was it really appropriate for a first date? She shrugged and stepped inside. Right away, she realized she didn't care. The scents in this café made her mouth water, and she nearly moaned out loud in pleasure. Well, damn. New favorite café indeed.

"Hi there! Welcome to The Frisky Bean. Have you been here before? Probably not, since I'd remember if you had and of course we've only been open for eight months, so quite new. What can I get for you?"

This was all said with such speed and exuberance, Shira nearly flinched. She had to wonder if this could still be her favorite new place with the overly cheery person working behind the counter. Was there a way to maybe avoid her? Order ahead? Her consternation with being overwhelmed with perkiness must have shown on her face because the woman with the stunning, messy, curly red hair grimaced and said with less exuberance, "Too much, huh?" Her voice dropped to nearly a whisper. "Sorry. You're obviously one of the people who needs some coffee defenses before I approach you. Let's try that again." And with a dramatically less excited almost comically even tone she said, "Is there something I can help you with?"

Comical it might be, but it worked. Shira was now ready to answer. "Sorry. Coffee first may as well be my motto, but so should, Oscar the Grouch was misunderstood." She winked, hoping to diffuse the tension she'd accidentally created. It seemed to have worked, as the woman behind the counter visibly relaxed. So she continued: "I'm meeting someone here. They should be arriving any minute. Do you have a menu I can look at until then?"

"Sure." The woman handed her a card and then continued, still in a friendly but calm tone, "My name is Summer. Let me know when you're ready to order."

"Thanks."

"No problem. Take your time."

As she perused the menu, Shira's eyes opened wide and she felt a blush creeping up her cheeks. That slogan on the window wasn't kidding around. A bell sounded behind her, but she was so engrossed in the menu items, she forgot to keep a look out for her date. She was oblivious until she heard a deep, sexy male voice coming from right next to her. "See something you like?" In fact, it came from too close. She reacted before she could think better of it, leaving her full of regrets the moment after.

CHAPTER TWO

Aaron Sanders couldn't believe his luck. He'd just decided to test his company's new app when his phone let him know someone was in his vicinity. And boy was she beautiful. Or maybe more: striking. In her picture, she had an olive complexion, long blackish-brown curly hair, and almond-shaped, dark brown eyes. Intense eyes. The image looked kind of like a professional headshot, and he wondered what she did for a living. Of course, there was always the possibility that she used a fake photo or that no one would come. He had to try, though. That was the point of his app.

If a person didn't show up, wasn't who they seemed, or there was no chemistry, you were only committing a short amount of time to each date. Just enough to grab a cup of coffee and then you could get back to your life. No exchange of phone numbers or addresses or emails. No commitment at all. And, if no one showed up, at least maybe you'd discovered a cool new spot, so not a total loss.

When he'd walked up to The Frisky Bean he had to admit to being a little concerned it had been included on the app because people might get weirded out at having a first date at such a provocative location. That was true only until he'd made his way inside. The place smelled incredible and had a very welcoming air about it. He noticed the eye-catching, pale, redhead standing behind the counter first and waved a hand at her in greeting, hoping to silence whatever she had been about to say. It worked, which was a good thing, because his eyes locked on the same hair he'd seen in the picture. The tresses crowned a soft, full-figured body with a deliciously rounded bottom. He liked an ass he could sink his teeth into. He was such an ass man.

At that moment, his date seemed preoccupied. She hadn't even turned toward him when he'd entered. While that stung his ego a bit, he was curious about what held her so completely enthralled.

He scanned the food items listed from over her shoulder and had to bite his tongue to keep from laughing. Instead he looked at her and saw the blush that colored her cheeks. Lovely. Her face was just as arresting in person. He really had hit the jackpot. His app was the best thing ever made. Clearly. Trying not to startle her, in his most soothing tone he leaned in and inquired, "See something you like?"

Not soothing enough apparently, because she startled anyway and slammed both of her palms into his chest. Hard. Since her reaction had caught him completely off guard, he toppled. It was almost worth the bruise to his butt and ego to see those amazingly expressive eyes grow round with the comical realization of what she'd just done. Somewhere in the background, his brain registered the exclamation of shock from the woman behind the counter, but he only had eyes for the woman in front of him, who reached to help him up.

"I'm so sorry! I can't believe I did that. But... You know... You really shouldn't stand so close to a woman when she isn't expecting it. You might find yourself facing a self-defense trainer who reacts decisively to such things."

"Yes. I think that lesson was just thrust into me. What a good instructor you are."

She snickered as he took her proffered hand and made his way to standing.

He continued, "Shall we try this again?"

"Yes. I suppose that would make more sense than slinking off and claiming an emergency embarrass-ectomy."

"I know which I prefer." He enjoyed the warmth that crept into her eyes as he smiled at her. "Hi. I'm Aaron and I would very much enjoy getting you whatever you want off of that highly inappropriate and yet enticing menu."

"I'm Shira and I would very much like a, um, Moaning Mocha." He appreciated the way her voice grew huskier and she looked at him directly, as she told him what she wanted. *Hot.*

He turned to the woman at the counter who was beaming at them. She seemed like the kind of person who was awfully chipper. Maybe she dipped into the coffee a little too much. She woke from her contemplation, straightening and talking with her hands as she said, "What can I get—ow!" One of her hands collided with the cash register next to her. She grimaced and scowled at the register but then continued, "—you?"

He looked over at Shira and saw her biting her slightly quivering lip. It was obvious she was trying not to laugh at the antics of the barista. He picked up a menu from the counter and said, "One Moaning Mocha, one Escapist Espresso, and, do you have any recommendations for a baked good to go with our drinks? What's good here?"

The cashier's face perked up. "Obviously, since I'm a co-owner, I have to say everything here is delicious, but our best seller is the Bondage Banana Bread also called the 3B. We also make killer scones. Right now we have the Rock-Your-Socks Blueberry Scones straight from the oven." She began pointing inside the display case and said, "We also have a few seasonal items right now, with the holidays around the corner. The Well-Hung Gingerbread Man, Peppermint Bark and Bite, Yule Cream My Log, Candy My Yam Muffin, Lace-Me-Up Latkes, and finally, Stripped Down Sufganiyot."

That was a lot of information. Shira must have thought so too, because when he looked over at her, her eyes seemed a little glazed over. She blinked a couple of times, looked back at him, then opened her mouth as if to say something, but closed it again.

From behind the counter he heard, "Oh no. I did it again. Sorry. How about I work on your drink orders and let you get back to me?"

"Sounds like a good idea. Thanks," he responded.

Shira suddenly smiled, and it was breathtaking. Her whole face lit up with just the small twist of her lips. She mock-whispered to him, "I think Summer is going to kick me out for my lack of perk soon."

Before he could ask who Summer was, the woman behind the counter yelled over the top of the steaming sound, "Never, my new grumpy friend."

They all began to crack up but he was completely transfixed by Shira's gregarious laugh. He guessed that she was reserved until, well, she wasn't. What else wasn't she reserved about? He found he wanted to know.

When she finally sobered, she said, "I'd like to try the two Hanukkah-themed items and I'm willing to share. How about you? Interested?"

Oh. He was interested. Very, very interested. Instead of responding, he turned back to Summer, and said, "One of the latkes, one of the sufganiyot, and one of the gingerbread men please."

"You like them well-endowed, too? Nice." He heard his date comment.

"I just thought you could take it with you to remember me by."

It took only a heartbeat for her to understand his meaning and she laughed again, and it was everything he hoped to achieve with that order. Music. Just lovely. His app was the absolute best for this encounter alone. A few minutes together and he was entranced.

CHAPTER THREE

Once Shira was able to catch her breath again, she said, "Well... that *is* a great alternative to the traditional dick pic." And then her amusement overcame her. Again. She had been ready for the worst but totally unprepared for the reality that was her blind date. Aaron was just as gorgeous in-person as his picture made him out to be. While that was a pleasant surprise, she was completely floored by his ability to make her laugh and his seemingly laid-back personality.

She still couldn't believe she'd knocked him down, but the ease with which he handled it was impressive. Also, considering the food they were ordering, his joke had been subtle, instead of getting downright dirty or leering like a teenager—also big bonus points. She was actually looking forward to sitting with him and getting to know him for the short time they had.

Aaron paid for their food after she tried to cover her half with no success. Ultimately, they agreed she could grab the next coffee. And... already talking about a next time worked just fine for her. They grabbed their drinks and headed to one of the two-person tables in the enjoyable café. The walls were a warm mustard yellow with risqué black and white photos for sale throughout. It was a perfect balance between inviting and sensual. Like a warm comforting hug from your lover that develops into an unexpected boner. The bonus boner.

What she found surprising was that she was suddenly tongue-tied. She dated plenty, but it had been a while since she'd gone on a blind date, and she wasn't sure what to talk about first. The ease with which they'd bantered just a minute ago gave way to normal first date insecurity. Luckily, Aaron didn't seem to suffer from the same problem.

"So. You're a self-defense instructor? Is that your day job?"

In the background she heard Summer putting together the rest of their order as she considered her answer.

"I am, but no, it's not my day job. I'm a blogger and freelance writer. So, Immedia-Date has found me a new place to work."

"Nice. What do you blog or write about?"

This is when things usually became awkward, because most guys would back off quick when they heard what she wrote about. Because she really liked Aaron, she decided to hedge. If things moved to a second date, she could always go into more detail then. "I blog about things in daily life, as well as offer reviews to my readers."

For a moment she wondered if he could tell she wasn't being completely forthcoming as he studied her instead of replying. Then it seemed he accepted her answer because his face relaxed, and he did respond. "You must be very good if that's your day job. It's quite a saturated market."

"I am." She wasn't being boastful. She was considered one of the best in her corner of the blogosphere, and she had the traffic and advertising dollars to prove it.

"Confident."

"You bet."

"I like that."

Warmth flooded her. So did she. "And you? What do you do?"

He seemed to pause again before he continued with, "I'm part of a startup that creates apps."

"And you're not located in Silicon Valley?"

"Why be in Silicon Valley when you can be in Silicon Beach?"

"Good point. Venice Beach has definitely changed a whole lot in recent years. Does that mean you're a surfer as well?"

"Oh. Absolutely."

"Sounds like we each have our side gigs."

"What's life without a little bit of this and a little bit of that?"

"Indeed." That came from Summer who walked up with several plates she placed between them. "I threw in our popular 3B for you to try for your first visit. Hopefully, we get to see you both in here from now on." She smiled at them and wandered off.

"Wow. It's not just the names." Shira studied each item before them.

"Do those latkes actually have a corset lacing design?" Aaron's voice was filled with awe.

"I think so. And wow, the bread really is tied up with that banana."

"And damn, sufganiyot holes to dip in six different toppings. Genius."

That was when they both looked at the gingerbread man, looked at each other, and began to laugh all over again, because really, it was all too much fun. Shira had experienced more pure enjoyment on this date in the first fifteen minutes than she had in the whole of some of her relationships. And wasn't that a sad state of affairs. Of course, that was exactly why she'd started blogging about dating and relationships. Now wasn't it?

They spent the next thirty minutes indulging in the decadent, delicious, and downright divine drink, food and conversation. It was Aaron who finally said, "I need to get back to work, but I want to see you again if you're interested."

Shira had to bite her lip to keep from shouting "Yes!" She took a breath and then with an even voice replied, "I'd like that too." Now she had to wonder, since she knew how these things often went, what route he would take. Exchange numbers and then keep her waiting for a few days before he reached out? Ask her for a date someday in the obscure future? Finish with, "I'll be in touch." She'd heard it all before. And maybe that made her just a bit too jaded, because that wasn't what he said at all.

"How about tonight? What are you doing later?"

It took her a beat to recover from her shock to answer, "I don't have any plans. I'd love to get together tonight."

The warmest smile spread across his handsome face. She'd gotten caught on just staring at that face during their brief time together. Chiseled chin covered with a seemingly permanent five o-clock shadow... His dark brown hair trimmed short in a classic style... And his eyes a stunning hazel... Now those eyes were shining with such warmth, along with his smile, and she sent a prayer up to whoever would listen that this was for real. He seemed like an answer to an unacknowledged wish from deep inside her fantasies.

She opened her phone and saw the app staring back at her and made a mental note to thank Keren's company with a review for coming up with Immedia-Date. Shira also needed to thank her friend for asking her to test it. Clicking away from the app, she brought up her contacts, and then handed Aaron her phone.

"Go ahead and put your information in here and I'll call you so you have mine."

She continued to let her eyes and soul feast as he did just that. After he called himself, he handed back her phone, and entered her information into his contacts. Then he tapped some more, and her phone vibrated.

She looked at the screen and she'd received a text from him. She smiled goofily and opened the message. It read:

How does dinner sound? I can be ready at six. How about you? And where should I pick you up? Or would you be happier meeting at the restaurant?

She thought about answering him directly, but it was too enticingly fun to play along. So she wrote back:

It's not a good sign if we are already both on our phones when we're together. Jumped straight from first date to married couple of thirty years. Sad. Sad. Sad. Wink emoji. I would prefer to meet at the restaurant for now. Just text me where and when, and I'll be there.

Their eyes caught and held after he read and replied to the message. Before she could see what he'd texted, he got up, leaned down, and pressed his rough, stubbled cheek to hers, causing all sorts of lusty sensations to course through her system as he whispered, "It's a date."

She was still sitting there, her body tingling, as Summer and a man she hadn't seen before sat down across from her. Where had the extra chair come from? She looked up at the other woman and expelled the breath she hadn't realized she was holding.

Summer leaned in and spoke in a loud whisper. "Well, that was something. Was it as good as it looked from over there?"

"Oh, yeah. I'd have to go with, better." She tentatively smiled at them both.

The new guy was a beautiful dark-brown, Black man with soulful, laughing eyes who was busy fanning himself. He leaned in conspiratorially and said, "If it was any better, we would need to spray you down with ice water. In fact, I may need to be sprayed down with ice water just watching you two. I'm Kevin, by the way. Co-owner and baker extraordinaire."

"Nice to meet you. And how does one go about eating what you make and looking like you do?"

He winked at her and answered even as Summer snorted. "Trade secret, honey."

Summer snorted again and said, "You're so full of shit. Simple answer. Luck, genetics, being too busy to actually indulge in eating much of what you make, and actually finding joy in being a gym rat." She nudged him and he winked back at her. Then Summer turned back to her, "Looked like you scheduled a second date?"

"Yep. Tonight."

"Awesome! You'll have to come back and tell us how it went. I think you're our first First Date. I feel really invested now. Like our very own live and in-person Blind Dates show."

"You do realize I'm not actually a reality TV show? Right? Buuut, if you want to know more about my dating life, follow my blog." Shira pulled out one of her cards and handed it to Summer, who read it out loud to Kevin.

"Rae Ramson. Bold Bitch Guide for Dating and Defense. Rae Ramson?" Summer looked up and tilted her head enquiringly.

"Altered version of my name. Pseudonym. I like having some anonymity."

"Of course. Consider me your newest follower."

"You know this bold bitch will be reading." Kevin confirmed, and then grimaced. "Assuming I have any time, that is. I may have to get the CliffsNotes from this one." He indicated Summer. "Planning, perfecting, and implementing all of our baked con-perfect-ions does not allow for much downtime."

A few minutes later and with a bagged well-hung gingerbread man in hand—to remember Aaron by, as if she could forget—Shira left her two new friends. She pulled out her phone as she approached her car to text Keren and was reminded that she still hadn't read the last thing Aaron had texted her before he left.

Maybe we'll get to see about that thirty year couple situation one day. It's been a true pleasure meeting you and I can't wait to see you tonight.

Warmth saturated every cell in her body, and she stood rooted as she reread the message four more times. Okay. Five. She finally entered her car and proceeded to text Keren.

Your app rocks! I met the greatest guy. I'll talk to you later, after he and I have our second date tonight. Wink emoji.

Nice! So happy it went well. Can't wait to hear more. Entering my meeting now. Give me the goods later.

Shira couldn't help but hope that there would be a lot of goods to share.

∽

Aaron waited anxiously for Shira to arrive. He'd chosen a delicious, casual Thai place he liked to frequent not too far from The Frisky Bean. Since he had no idea where Shira lived, he figured he'd take a chance she wouldn't have to travel too far if he stayed in the same basic area. Her last text said she was on her way. Since he'd left first that morning, he had no idea what kind of car he should watch for.

He couldn't remember ever feeling as nervous about a date as he was for this one. Something about Shira told him that this was going to be life-altering. He would have said it was ridiculous to feel like that after knowing someone for only an hour. Yet, he was sure deep down that his life was about to head in a new direction.

He saw lights pulling into the parking lot, then shut down as a car parked. Was it her? His hands got a little clammy and he was forced to roll his eyes at himself. *You're a fucking CEO dammit. Clammy hands? Really?* He quickly dried them on his pants as he saw a vision walking toward him.

Shira had changed from earlier in the day and was now wearing a pair of skinny jeans that had to have been painted on her and heeled, calf-climbing boot. He couldn't tell what she sported on top because she wore a black, form-fitting jacket. Her hair was still down, though, and her curls bounced with every step. The lights along the parking lot illuminated her face and even from a bit of a distance, he could see she wore red lipstick. He was screwed.

He calmed his racing heart and covertly adjusted his pants. He was ready when she opened the glass door and came in with her sexy red smile. "Hi. I hope this place is to your liking. You look beautiful." The last he said as he leaned down and allowed himself a press of their cheeks and air kisses in welcome. She probably didn't realize just how much he loved the smell of her. In fact, he couldn't get her sweet scent out of his mind the whole time he'd been in his meeting, earlier. And now he used their welcoming moment to inhale her once again.

"Hi. I love this place, actually. I don't live too far from here."

"Wow. Me either. Wouldn't it be funny if we were neighbors?"

"Funny or creepy? I guess depending on how tonight goes, we shall see which it is." she winked.

When the host indicated, he ushered her into a booth and they both placed their orders. When the green tea arrived, he lifted his glass in toast. "I have a good feeling about tonight. So perhaps we can toast to new possibilities?"

She raised her glass as well and said, "To new possibilities, surprising compatibilities, and hopeful opportunities."

"Well said. L'chaim." He reached out his cup and she clinked hers to his.

"L'chaim."

Had they just sealed some sort of deal? Some sort of fate? It felt like they had, and he was—surprisingly—totally okay with that. His only unease was knowing he hadn't been completely forthcoming about what he did. There would be time for that, though. Right?

No matter how sure he felt, he needed to see that he wasn't just infatuated. That there was substance to his sudden feelings. Maybe on their next date, if there was one, would be the right time to share that information. Not tonight. Tonight was for getting to know each other.

CHAPTER FOUR

Shira: *How is it possible that the best date I've ever been on ends with just a kiss. I mean. It was a helluva kiss, but still. Have I lost my touch that much? <sigh> I did have the best night ever. Conversation along with flirtation flowed so easily with him. We decided to focus on who we are instead of work, which was great for me, since I still haven't told him what I blog about, maybe next time, and he was just as amazing as at the coffee shop. There is too much more to share in text. Buy why just a kiss?!?! Cry emoji.*

Keren: *Sounds both fantastic and frustrating. You poor, poor thing. A guy who shows you an amazing time and respects you. My heart bleeds.*

Shira: *Your sarcasm is unwelcome and noted, young lady. I may just not tell you at all. You'll have to just read about my dating life on my blog like everyone else.*

Two weeks later:

Keren: *You're really going to make me keep reading about your new guy on your blog? Seven dates in two weeks?!? This sounds like it's really getting serious. I can't talk until this weekend, but you better be on my phone this Saturday. You hear me?*

Shira: I hear you. Honestly, I would have called, but between your schedule, my schedule, and the dates, I haven't had time for a call. Seven dates. Seven dates and no sex. The best dates ever and no sex. I'll need to have that conversation on Saturday if for no other reason than for you to confirm that I'm not imagining the attraction between him and me because I am so ready and he keeps giving me devastating kisses that lead absolutely nowhere. Can't he respect me in the morning instead?

Friday Night:

Shira was losing her ever-loving mind. Okay. Most people might hold off on sex for longer than two weeks, but those people hadn't had seven of the most wonderful, romantic, funny, and sexy dates that had ever been dated. Not to mention, there was nothing wrong with getting intimate quick if both parties were onboard. It just gave that much more data to decide if they were compatible, really. And so far, she and Aaron were about as compatible as two people could be, so why? Why wouldn't he sleep with her?

They'd even already made plans to celebrate Hanukkah with each of their families in three weeks. In fact, they'd already placed an order for sexy, fun food from The Frisky Bean to bring along to both parties. With everything being so good, why weren't they sleeping together? Or even getting to second base? Was she that unattractive to him? Maybe he liked everything else about her but didn't like her like that? A convenient Jewish girlfriend for the holidays? It didn't feel that way.

Then why?

Well, tonight, she was going to make a bold move and see where that got her. Forget waiting around for him to do it or getting shut down when she tried to gently press. She would make her play, and if he still wasn't interested, then they would need to have a little talk.

Everything else was going so well. She hadn't felt this connected to another person before. Well, except for the fact that she still hadn't gotten around to telling him about the specifics of her blog… But they always found so many more interesting things to talk about. And maybe she was being a bit of a chicken shit. Probably, but she would tell him soon.

She was more concerned at the moment with whether he was attracted to her. The press of his hard cock through his pants always said yes, but his brushing her off after melting her panties with kisses at the end of each date said maybe not.

She was so confused but things would change tonight. Shira checked her purse and yes, the condoms she'd bought for their second date were still there. She looked around her place and yep, everything was relatively tidy, and her bed was ready for mayhem of the best kind. Tonight, she was going to be the bold bitch she billed herself as being. Sex or a deep conversation about it. One way or another she would understand what was holding them back. The eighth date would be the charm.

∼

AARON COULDN'T BELIEVE HOW GREAT THINGS WERE GOING WITH Shira. His balls couldn't believe what an idiot he was.

How hadn't they slept together yet? He knew why, though, even if his balls weren't too keen on the events, or lack thereof. He had never liked another woman more, and yet he hadn't come clean about owning the company that made Immedia-Date. At first he didn't tell her because he thought it might be weird for him to be using his own app. But after how great things were going, it felt creepy he hadn't told her to begin with. The longer he went without saying something, of course, the weirder and creepier it got. Why hadn't he just told her when they met?

He knew, though. It wasn't just that he was using his own app. Women always treated him differently once they found out he was the CEO of a successful startup. Especially one that made dating apps. Immedia-Date was just the latest in a string of apps he had developed to help people get together in the modern age. He didn't want Shira to like him for being a CEO or dislike him for his dating apps. Sometimes, people who had a bad date that originated on one of his apps blamed the app. Matching algorithms could only do so much, and there were no miracles.

Well, at least, that was true most of the time. But Aaron had begun to believe he had exactly that kind of miracle. Shira was everything he had ever looked for in a potential partner. He assumed from their kisses that she might also be everything he was looking for in a lover. Of course, since he was uncomfortable sleeping with her without telling her the truth, and he kept avoiding the truth because of how wonderful a time they were having...

Well, shit. He was being ridiculous. Time to get off this roller-coaster and just confess. Tonight. He'd see just how far she wanted to go, if at all, once he told her the truth.

It was almost time to pick up Shira. By date two, she had given him her address, which—as she'd said—wasn't far from where they originally met. It wasn't far from where he lived, either, though thinking about that made him cringe. He'd been hedging about his home because if she saw his place, it would be clear he wasn't completely forthcoming about his position in the company. If she came in, she'd see things with his company logo.

He'd been brought up better than this. Shame flushed through him.

Tonight he would clear everything up and hope he didn't lose her in the process.

CHAPTER FIVE

Shira's heart thudded loudly in her ears when the knock sounded at her door. Why was she so fucking nervous? *Pull yourself together. You don't even plan on jumping him until later. For now, this is just like any other date.* Her pep talk did nothing for her. Her fingertips were all tingles as she opened the door. He was so beautiful. She wanted to pull him by the neck of his shirt into her house right now and play naked tackle football. Clearly her libido was out of control.

She tried for nonchalant humor when she spoke, but failed miserably. Her voice came out much deeper and huskier than intended. Her "Hi stranger," took on a very seductive, role-play-like nature, instead of the joke she'd intended. His intense perusal of her body as he didn't answer made it clear he had heard it as well.

Don't panic!

His gaze felt like a caress running from her strappy sandals, up her mid-thigh length form fitting dress, all the way to her heaving (*Was she heaving? Oh God! She was heaving.*) breasts. She was going to hyperventilate if something didn't happen, and soon. Well, fuck this.

She reached out, grabbed his shirt collar and did what she'd wanted when she first saw him. He was inside, door closed, and playing tongue tango with her in an instant. And he was definitely participating. *Yes!*

Maybe they weren't going out tonight after all. Now was as good a time as any. Carpe diem and all that jazz. Their kisses during their past dates were hot. But not just hot. More like H-A-W-T *hawt*. This kiss? This kiss put all those kisses in the kiddie pool. This kiss was scorched earth. He absolutely devastated her when he began to devour her lips with his.

He was firm and demanding and she yielded everything to him. At least at first. But she was not just a giver, she was also a taker and so when her senses came back online a few minutes later, she began to press her own kisses back at him, nipping and sucking on his bottom lip like she imagined doing to other parts of his anatomy. He groaned as she did, with clear invitation for more.

At that point, Shira was ready for anything. Wall? Couch? Bed? Clothes on? Clothes off? She really didn't care. She just wanted to feel every inch of the hard length poking her through their clothes pumping hard inside of her. She would beg if he needed her to. Did he enjoy begging? She could do some damn fine sexual begging. Of course, she could also make him beg, but that might have to wait for another time. She was too far gone in lust to play at that game tonight. She was ready dammit. Anything!

Except him backing away.

She practically fell to the floor, because her knees went weak. She braced herself with a hand against the wall and thought maybe he'd backed up to position them somewhere else, or look for a condom, or something else along those lines. One look at his face and it was clear that wasn't it at all.

What had she done wrong? Had she moved too fast? Well fuck him, if that was it. She was a modern woman. If she wanted sex, she wasn't going to be shamed by anyone for being clear about what she wanted.

She didn't see condemnation in his eyes, though. Before she spoke and made things worse by jumping to conclusions, she observed him and waited for him to say something, because what she did see there was trepidation. Was he breaking up with her? That couldn't be it after that kiss, could it?

She needed to take control of her damn imagination. She decided to help him spit it out with a question, instead of any accusations or suspicions. "What's wrong?"

He finally looked up, met her eyes, and said, "I have something I need us to talk about before we take this—" he waved between them, clearly indicating their bodies "—further."

"Sounds rather ominous. Should I sit down or are you planning on leaving soon?"

"I'm sorry. I don't mean to make it sound bad. I hope you don't think it is, and I don't plan on leaving. Unless I'm asked to."

"Okay. Then let's sit down."

She turned from the door and within a few steps, she was sitting on her couch. He followed and sat next to her, turned toward her, and grabbed her hands in his. Sheesh. Didn't he know this position never meant anything good was coming? All the movies and TV shows taught you that. Nervousness permeated her being and infiltrated the air around her. The room felt even smaller than usual, and it was hard to breathe.

"Just tell me, because it can't be worse than the anticipation you're creating."

"I know you're right. I just feel kind of stupid about it all. Okay. Here's the deal. I haven't been completely up front with you about what I do. And I didn't want to sleep with you until there was nothing but honesty between us."

Well, shit. Apparently, he was a more upstanding guy than she was girl because she hadn't been upfront about what she did either, and she had no qualms about wanting to sleep with him. She flushed with embarrassment and that seemed to confuse him so she rushed to admit her own shame. "Um, funny you should mention that. I haven't been totally upfront with you either."

∼

AARON WASN'T SURE WHAT REACTION HE'D EXPECTED. AFTER THAT entryway mauling from them both, he'd known it was now or never, and he really didn't want to ruin everything by going in with a lie. What he definitely had not been expecting was that she had a confession to make as well. The absurdity of it all hit him and there was no preventing the laughter that broke out.

Of course, expressing amusement in the face of someone's confession was usually not the right thing to do, but this was why he felt—even after such a short time—that they were meant for each other. Across from him, Shira was loudly entertained. Lovely. All the horrible tension that had built up around them in the wake of their make-out session diffused almost completely.

In the aftermath, Shira wiped away tears from laughing so hard, and he was relaxed and ready to talk. "What a pair we make."

"Yes. Apparently. Who goes first?"

"I will. Since I started it." He snorted. "Quite literally. You see, I own the company that created Immedia-Date."

Her eyes got big and her hands tensed in his. "You what? Could you repeat that?"

He thought he'd been done being nervous until she reacted with total shock at his pronouncement. *Fuck.* "I'm the CEO of the company that made the dating app we used to meet each other."

"Huh. That's what I thought you said."

She looked pensive and didn't speak for a while, and his anxiety started to rise with each passing heartbeat. He really had fucked this up. He was about to say, "I can explain," which, of course, he couldn't, not really, but it was the kind of thing you always said when trying to salvage a relationship. Before he could stick his foot in his mouth, though, she began to talk.

"Do you know Keren Sabinski?"

"Um. Yes. Why?" Not what he expected.

"She's the reason we're here today. She's one of my best friends and she asked me to test her company's, well, *your* company's latest app for her when she had to bail on a get-together." She paused, staring off into the distance. Then...she giggled.

He hoped that her amusement was a good sign, but he wasn't ready to drop his wariness just yet. It would be best to get some direction from her about the turn in their conversation. He asked. "And that's funny?"

"It is when you realize that the only reason you and I met was because some birds shit-bombed Keren."

He had to laugh too. He remembered walking into the meeting that first day he'd met Shira and seeing a disorganized Keren with wet hair, which wasn't what he was used to from her. "I wondered about that at the meeting that day. Her wet hair and all."

"Yes. I'm sure, knowing her, she washed her hair at least ten times."

His heart stopped racing and his fingers, which he hadn't realized had started gripping her hands too tight, relaxed. One of the reasons he'd fallen so hard for this woman was because she had a quick mind and a relaxed nature. Whenever they stumbled onto topics they couldn't agree on, it was very easy to debate with each other but ultimately, to walk away comfortable with not agreeing. Of course, they agreed on the important things, but knowing how to argue with someone—he'd learned from his parents—was one of the tricks that lead to a long, happy relationship. If this was any indication, they argued well. Still, he hedged. "We okay?"

Her eyes startled to his, and her brows were drawn. "Of course. Why would I care if you're the CEO of that company or any other? I assume you didn't tell me because it would have been awkward, which is a great segue into my confession."

"Oh? Are you the CEO of a company too?" When she smiled, he took it as a reward for trying to lighten the mood. That smile was what he wanted to see each morning and night and many times in-between. He knew things were moving fast, but he was pretty sure he was in love with her. Saying that would *definitely* be moving too fast, so he kept it to himself.

"I *am* a blogger. I write about dating and self-defense. Most guys freak out when they hear that I share information about my dating life, so I tend to keep that detail to myself."

He had hoped to take her news as easily as she had his, but he had to admit that he was taken aback. "Have you written about us?" Clearly his anger showed on his face, or in his tone, or both because she looked hurt and yanked her hands from his as she stood up and faced him. She was closing down. All her innate openness and humor from a moment before? Gone. He hated it, but he also hated thinking about his life being used as fodder for gossip. "Without asking me first?"

"And this is why I don't tell anyone. Yes, I have. If you understood me at all, you wouldn't be so upset. You would trust me not to do something to hurt you. But, maybe you don't. Maybe I've been deluding myself with how close we've gotten in such a short time. So... If you need to leave, then go."

CHAPTER SIX

Shira began to pace. She couldn't believe it was happening again with Aaron. She had been so sure of him, of them, just a short while ago. Hell, she hadn't even cared and even *understood* why he hadn't told her about his true occupation. But now he couldn't do the same for her? He was going to react like every other guy?

They never bothered to check what she wrote, they just got upset that she wrote about them at all. The least someone could afford her was the courtesy of getting mad about something she actually did. Not some imagined offense. Fuck it. If he wanted to leave, fine.

She crossed her arms over her chest and faced him. She knew it was a defensive pose, but she was feeling damn defensive. He wasn't looking at her, though. He was looking down at his hands, which were still in the position she had left them when she pulled away. It made it look like he 'd been holding something precious that had slipped through his fingers.

She was right here. He didn't have to let her go.

He finally looked up and spoke, his expression closed off. "I don't want to leave. Will you tell me your blog name so I can read it for myself?"

Holy shit. He actually *did* want to do his research. She fought to keep her hope tempered, because there was every likelihood that this still ended badly for her. "Yes. It's called Bold Bitch Guide for Dating and Defense."

He quirked an eyebrow at the name and smirked even as he entered it on his phone. "I thought it was a bad thing to call a woman a bitch."

"Guys should never use it without permission, but women have reclaimed the word and affectionately use it with each other."

"Noted."

As she watched him search for her site, she began pacing again. What else was she going to do? Oh wait. That's right. Wine. She was going to do wine.

She went into the kitchen and grabbed a couple of glasses. She poured a helping of her latest Wine-of-the-Month bottle of pinot noir into each, and came back, putting one on the coffee table near Aaron and nursing her own as she continued pacing. How long could it take to read about seven dates? Well, eight, if you counted The Frisky Bean. So perhaps this was their ninth date?

For some reason an image of a fully lit hanukkiah flashed through her mind. It was warm and full of light. An indication of miracles. She wasn't sure why that popped into her head, but she did know she was hoping for a miracle. She didn't want things to end for them. She also loved what she did and would not apologize for it.

She paused to take a sip of wine and stared out one of her windows into the night. He must have moved quite silently, because even as she realized she was staring at his reflection behind hers, she felt his arms close around her, his chin resting gently over her shoulder, bringing him cheek to cheek with her. She held her breath, air a commodity she wasn't trading in at the moment.

"You are an amazing writer. I admit, I had a lot of concerns when I began to read, but, I have to say, I fell for you, for us, all over again reading your words." She felt more than saw his smirk, with the bunching of his cheek next to hers. "And you gave our app quite the review. We wondered why there was an uptick in sales at the end of last week. Thank you."

She relaxed back into his body, and the cold that only the wine had kept at bay was banished in the heat radiating off of him, body and spirit. "You're welcome. Are...Are we good?"

"Honey, we are more than good. We are great."

She closed her eyes with relief and took a deep breath, taking in the scent of him all around her. She reached her hand out, placing her glass on the nearby bookshelf before spinning in his arms to face him. She fought the tears that threatened to overflow. So much emotion and tension and anxiety and relief left her feeling a bit unbalanced. She'd started the night wanting to have sex with her hot boyfriend. Casual fun.

Now, after all they revealed and accepted about each other and the emotional connection they formed, she wanted to create an intimate physical bond. All her defenses were down and her soul called out to his.

His responded.

She felt the link in her very bones.

Their mouths met in the middle of the sweetest kiss they had ever shared. Unlike the blazes and bonfires of before, this was a slow burn, like a match prepared to set a candle ablaze. The kiss deepened and morphed by slow, deliberate degrees. Shira was a total goner. She knew it. And while she wasn't ready to say it, she was oh so ready to show it.

To feel it.

To feel him.

To feel them.

Aaron swooped her up into his arms and started toward the back of her place, where he must have assumed her bedroom was. He was right, of course, because there really was nowhere else to go, but she said, "Wait!"

Concern flashed through his eyes, "If you aren't ready for this—"

"No! I am!" She may have said that a little too enthusiastically, but whatever. She was. "I just need to grab the condoms from my purse."

A sexy grin came over his face, and he said, "Why don't we start with the two I stuffed into my wallet since that's already on me?"

She couldn't help but smile back. "Two sounds like a good beginning."

"How many times do you plan to take advantage of me exactly?"

She cupped his cheek with one hand and wrapped the other around the back of his neck, leaning up to whisper in his ear, "As many as I can."

He gave a mock-suffering sigh, but she felt a shiver as it ran down his spine, as he crossed the threshold into her bedroom.

"Be gentle with me." he joked.

"We'll see."

"Evil vixen. I bet you even ate poor, well-hung Aaron's pecker off. Didn't you?"

She gasped and then laughed even as he dumped her—not placed, but *dumped* her—on her bed. "Of course I did!"

Aaron ran a hand down the length of her leg, from the hem of her dress to her foot, causing every nerve to come to attention. He lifted her foot to his lips and placed a soft kiss on the inside of her ankle. Then, he slowly removed that strappy sandal and dropped it to the floor. He continued nuzzling the inside of that leg a little while longer, but eventually lifted the other leg to do the same.

She was left to watch him and feel him and moan. Every scrape of his chin against the sensitive skin of her inner calf made her breath hitch. She was so focused on the sensations he was evoking, she hadn't even realized she'd left her first foot on top of his shoulder. She wasn't aware until he had both of her legs propped up and began to lean forward, pushing her knees up towards her chest. What was he doing? He wasn't going to...oh...he was.

Aaron skimmed his face along the inside of her knees, against her thighs, inching her knees ever closer to her chest. He opened her in such a way that the hem of her skirt posed no protection from his hungry eyes on her black, lace-clad pussy. Wet lace-clad pussy. And getting wetter by the eye full.

As his face got within an inch of said soaked lace, he inhaled. "I can tell how turned on you are by this musk alone. So fucking hot." He pushed his face into the lace, kissing her through it.

"Aaron." His name came out a plea because she needed him to touch her. She reached her hand down and ran her fingers into his hair, delighting in the silky softness of it. "Please lick me. I want your mouth on me."

"Your wish is...something I'll be doing soon."

"What happened to 'my command?'" She gasped as he rubbed his nose along her clit, through the lace, which gave the caress a slight rough, scraping sensation.

"Right now, I command."

Fuck yeah. Her heart rate sped up even more.

She whimpered at the cold rush of air as he finally moved her underwear to the side and blew. She barely had time to register her sudden transition from warm to cold before she moved on to hot because his lips and tongue began caressing and sucking her pussy lips and clit. She arched up on a moan of pure pleasure as he settled in and began to feast.

This was not going to take long. She wasn't usually this quick to orgasm, but with how hot he had made her every night they'd gone out, she'd been edging for two weeks, refusing to take care of it by herself.

She usually did. That's why Magic Wands were invented after all. But something made her want to wait. Something instinctual told her that since he generated the lust, he should be the one to address it. On top of that, she knew it would be that much better if she waited. And damn, it was.

Before long, her insides coiling tighter and tighter, she was prepared to explode in spasms. When she got oh-so-close, he placed two fingers inside her opening with a gentle but firm thrust. Then he curled them, hitting her G-spot even as he sucked her clitoris. The pleasure arched her straight off the bed, gasping, "Aaron!" as she shook and came.

∼

AARON LOVED HER RESPONSIVENESS AND HER TASTE. SHIRA WAS simply exquisite. He gave her a moment to relax as he leaned back and began to yank his clothes off. He was ready for some skin-to-skin contact. He made sure to place the condoms on the nightstand before throwing his pants into the pile of clothes he'd made.

He felt—before he saw—her eyes on him. It felt like an actual caress running down his abdomen and straight to his engorged and bouncing cock. His cock that was so ready... Even now the tip was wet with precum. He was about to sit Shira up so he could pull her dress from her, when she flipped to her stomach, facing him, and took hold of his penis at the root. All he could do was helplessly groan as he watched her tongue dart to lick that precum from him. He was about to tell her to save the oral for another time, but he was too late.

Her mouth engulfed the head of his cock in warm heat, and it was all he could do not to thrust farther in. The pleasure her mouth gave him was intense, especially with her taste still tripping along his tongue.

But he was not going to come in her mouth. Not now. He had other plans and they involved him, a condom, and lots and lots of thrusting. Toward that goal, he threaded his fingers into her hair and held her immobile, pulled his dick away. She looked about to protest, but he didn't give her the chance. Instead, he pulled her to her knees, stripped her bare, and finally stared at the gorgeous body he'd been dreaming about for two weeks.

"If you plan to just watch, I'll go ahead and get started." She lay back, wrapping her hands around her full breasts. She squeezed and rubbed and pinched and he was torn, because the view really was that good, but that would have to wait for another day as well. He wanted her too badly to wait.

Aaron stretched out beside her. Accepting her breasts in sacrifice, he leaned down and sucked one nipple into his mouth, grasping the other with her hand trapped between his fingers. He sucked and he squeezed and he gently scraped teeth and nails over her pert nipples. He came up for air and then kissed her mouth so hard and thoroughly that she practically purred when he pulled away.

"Where do you think you're going?" she huskily asked.

He reached for the nightstand, for the condom, and came back triumphantly brandishing it. He waggled his eyebrows.

"You goofball!" she joked.

"I don't know about a goofball, but I definitely want to get my balls involved."

She grabbed the condom from him. "Turn over."

He laid back as Shira opened and positioned the condom, pinching the tip while rolling the rest onto his very hard shaft.

Once the condom was on, he couldn't remain passive. He pushed her to her back once again and kissed her, invading her mouth even as his dick slowly glided into her opening. She raised her legs against his hips and her wetness drove him smoothly into her snug warmth. She moaned directly into his mouth, and he swallowed it up like a prize.

This was the connection he'd known they both needed, so he stayed still, fully seated inside her, allowing them both to experience it. To enjoy his fullness engulfed by her softness. "You feel incredible."

"So do you."

Being inside Shira was like coming home. It was where he wanted to return anytime. Every time. But his cock had been patient enough the last couple of weeks. He needed to move. He looked Shira directly in her eyes as his hips shifted and began a slow, easy rhythm.

They were both so, so ready. His thrusts grew faster and deeper until he drove her to the edge again. He leaned back and drew one of her hands to his mouth sucking her fingers. Getting them nice and wet. "Show me how you like it."

It was obvious she understood him, because without hesitation, she reached between them and began to rub her clit, swiping back and forth. He watched for a minute, noting she preferred a side-to-side motion instead a more circular one, and then resumed his thrusts harder and deeper still. Her face was completely flushed, her body damp from sweat, and she had never looked more beautiful. He felt her spasms around his cock as she arched and called out his name and his control abandoned ship. Aaron lost himself in sensation, and finding his own climax soon after. As he was coming down, he held her close. They were both breathing heavily, and he closed his eyes in gratitude that neither of their confessions had ruined what they'd found.

∼

Saturday

Shira: *I'm banging your boss, bitch. Epic-ly so. Think you have time for a phone call now?*

Shira's phone rang.

CHAPTER SEVEN

Shira thought that Hanukkah with her family was a blast, but they had nothing on the Sanders. Aaron's family decorated the whole house as though for Christmas but with dreidel lights, blue and white lights, and a giant inflatable hanukkiah in the front yard. Who knew they had those?

She actually wasn't the only one from her family taking in all of the chaos as his nieces and nephews ran around. When his mom had heard that they planned to go celebrate with her family before coming over, they'd welcomed her small clan. Neither Shira nor Aaron were sure it was a great idea, but the parents had somehow gotten on the phone with each other, made all the arrangements, and conned, err... convinced them into it.

They were probably thoroughly screwed. Shira looked into the dining room and saw her mom in deep conversation with Aaron's mom. That was evidence enough that she was right, so she asked, "How screwed are we?"

Aaron, who was sitting next to her, whispered back, "I can't decide if it would have worried me more if they hadn't gotten along or that they're getting along so well."

"I'm leaning toward the latter myself. Think we can make a run for it?"

"No way. They'll just call and let us know they gave birth to us and we better get our butts back here."

Clearly their moms were cut from a similar cloth. She'd definitely heard lines like that before. She looked into the kitchen where both dads were putting the final touches on their dishes. She teased, "Will you be cooking for me, too?"

"Of course. My dad always taught me that a woman would do anything for a man who could cook. I took that to heart. I've even gone to some formal classes to up my game." He winked at her, and her heart wanted to skip right out of her chest and land in his hand.

Everyone started shuffling into the living room to open presents before they sat down to eat, which was apparently the Sanders' tradition. She and Aaron stood and helped in distributing gifts all around.

She was enjoying herself quite a lot. It was actually rather fun to have so much family around. She only had one brother, and he was currently studying abroad in Israel. She missed him, terribly. Maybe it wasn't a bad thing that their parents got along well? Only time would tell.

Aaron's sister, Rebecca, had already asked to join her at the gym where she taught self-defense. His divorced brother, Elijah, was hitting her up for dating advice in the modern age. And his last brother, Zach, along with his wife, Sarah, were asking Aaron and her to babysit. How had her life become so full, so fast? She wasn't totally sure.

At least she wasn't until she turned around to see if anyone else was missing a present. She found Aaron in front of her on one knee, holding a small box, and looking at her with utter devotion. Yeah. That's how it happened.

She tried not to freak out too much, but she couldn't control the tears that spilled down her cheeks. She thought over the last five weeks and they were the best, most life-altering weeks of her life. The last two, in fact, they'd basically been living together minus an official move in. If someone had told her she'd be okay with what was happening, before she met Aaron, she would have laughed. Now... elation like she'd never known was the only thing she was feeling.

Her adored was saying something really profound and it had to do with how she was his Hanukkah miracle or something like that. Something about how he knew it was fast but something, something and he'd never been surer of anything.

"Yes!" was running over and over through her mind along with, "Stop talking and ask me already!" until the end of his speech, when he said, "I love you."

She was so transfixed by that last part, she forgot about her first two thoughts. She also forgot to answer. It wasn't until he raised his brows at her in expectation that she realized it was her turn to talk. She got down on her knees so they could be eye-level when she said what she had to say. She looked directly into his beloved eyes and somehow croaked out, "I love you, too. And it's a definite yes."

She barely registered the cheers and well wishes all around them, because her whole world had narrowed down to one moment, one person, and one feeling. Their time, him, and the love flowing between them was all she knew. He captured her hand and slipped a ring onto her finger but she still couldn't look away. He put down the box and framed her face in both of his hands and kissed her. A gentle, sweet, barely-a-press-of-their-lips kiss, and it carried the message they both felt completely.

It was perfection. Until one of Aaron's nephews loudly exclaimed, "Eeeewwwww!" Everyone laughed. The spell she'd fallen under was broken even as her connection to Aaron had never been stronger.

She wasn't a fool. They might be moving too fast, but they could always have a long engagement. Alternately, her parents had only known each other for a month before they were engaged. And despite that, they'd been together for thirty-four years and were still a very happy, affectionate couple. Sometimes, you really do know when it's right.

This was right. This was where she belonged. This was love. And wasn't everyone a little bit foolish for love? Was there any other way to do it? She didn't think so.

Aaron leaned in and whispered in her ear, "What are you thinking about, my love? You have an interesting look on your face."

She whispered back, "I think we're very lucky to have all this love around us. I'm also lamenting having so many around us because I'm a little frisky. You think you'll have a living-version well-hung gingerbread man for me later? I think I fell in love with you for that trick."

His eyes grew heated as she spoke, and he leaned in like he liked to do, brushing his cheek along hers whispering, "It's a date."

∽

LATER THAT NIGHT, AARON LOOKED DOWN AT HIS FIANCÉ AND couldn't control his stupid grin of delight. She'd wanted to eat her gingerbread man up, and she had. She had taken him in her mouth within minutes of entering his—soon to be their—home and she refused to let go until he'd come, hard, down her greedy throat. She looked back at him, now, like the cat that had eaten the cream, and he knew he was one very lucky man.

"Happy now?" he asked.

"Oh yeah."

"Me too, love, but I'm far from satisfied. Come here."

She stood up, with his hand for assistance, and wrapped her arms around his neck. He kissed her deeply enjoying the taste of himself in her mouth. When he broke away, he had to ask, just to be sure. "Are you positive that you like the ring? We could always exchange it."

"Would you stop? I love the ring." She held it up as if to show it off. "I honestly hadn't expected you to remember how I felt about diamonds versus other stones, considering how many topics we covered over the course of our dates. But you did. And it's absolutely perfect."

His find sat on her ring finger. It was a delicate but decorative band with small inlaid stones like tiger's eye, onyx and lapis lazuli. Eight bits in total that formed a colorful mosaic of a figure eight, an infinity symbol. He could have afforded something big and flashy, but he'd known instantly when he'd laid his eyes on that ring, it was the right one.

Pleased at the pleasure he heard in her voice, he was ready to get back to *their* satisfaction. "I'm still hungry myself, love. It's time for you to give me my dessert." He could actually see the shivers of anticipation that coursed through her.

"That sounds divine."

"Come. I need you to ride my face and then, I plan to give you a massage. I can't slack off just because you've said yes."

"Definitely not."

A few hot, sweaty, and intensely connected hours later, Aaron could finally claim satisfaction for them both. They lay in bed, he on his back, one arm around her, with her head pillowed on his shoulder and her arm thrown across his abdomen.

Every night. He wanted this to last every night.

EPILOGUE

Bold Bitch Guide for Dating and Defense

Hey bitches,

For those of you who celebrate... Happy Hanukkah!

If you have been following along on this blog, you know that I recently used a dating app to find my Mr. Right. If you've been keeping up on our shenanigans, a.k.a., dates, you'll have watched our decent into madness, I mean love. Wink emoticon.

I have some Bold Bitch news for you all...

We got engaged last night. I hope you enjoy the picture of the ring. I forgot to look at it for thirty minutes after he slipped it on my finger. What can I say, I was distracted by my sexy fiancé. That word sounds so crazy, but it's true.

Some of you may be wondering what will happen with this blog. I know I would. Well, actually I did. Then I realized three things.

1. I have only ever scratched the surface on all my wacky dating stories. I have reserves for years, and I'll be sharing them all with you. More importantly, though...
2. People in committed relationships need to remember to keep dating each other, to allow the initial flame that brought them together to continue to burn throughout their lives. I plan to share tips and tricks on how to keep dating your significant other. And...
3. Self-defense and kicking ass will never go out of style, bitches.

IN HONOR OF FOOLISH, FAST, BUT UNDENIABLE LOVE, MY ADVICE today is to keep your heart open and seize opportunities to try, because you never know what path brings you together with the person you could love and be loved by. And when you do find that person, hang on and enjoy the ride.

MY HANUKKAH MIRACLE WAS FINDING AND FALLING IN LOVE WITH my man in eight dates (not to mention getting engaged a few weeks later). But miracles can't happen if you don't put in the effort to try.

STAY BOLD.

Rae

Coming in 2022, Frisky Intentions, the first full-length novel in the Frisky Bean series. Life heats up for Summer. Pre-order here.

EXCERPT OF FRISKY INTENTIONS

Summer

"Oh my god. That's so good." I moaned, swiping at the cream escaping my mouth. "You gave me a mouthgasm."

"Don't I always?"

"Yes, yes, you do."

"Yes, I do, now get your ass in gear, because we only have time for a quickie this morning."

I took one more bite of the decadent new confection, pointedly ignoring my best friend and co-owner of our café, Kevin Johnson. Unlike what my mama taught me, I spoke around my mouthful of sweet, delectable mana.

"If you wanted me to be quick, you shouldn't have handed me such taste-bud-stroking goodness as soon as I walked in the kitchen."

I cringed at his downright insulted look.

"Summer Palmer, it's like you don't even know me. When have I ever done anything less than a full, sensual enticement of the senses? I'm not risking the wrath of your nana Winnie. That woman taught us well, and there's no way I'd insult her by doing anything 'just good.' You know she always said—"

I joined in with him, reciting what Nana Winnie had taught us. I couldn't resist. "Food is love, and baked food is love with a kiss." Nana was so right. I felt it every time I got to baking. That special connection between me and the person enjoying my efforts filled me with all the best feels. I knew Kevin felt the exact same way. It's why we worked so well together.

Annnnnd... since he had a point, I tipped my head in agreement and apology. This was our dream, after all. Each day that I stepped into the kitchen with Kevin and was enveloped by the scent of warm baked goodness, I was transported back to when we were kids. We'd spent endless hours learning from Nana Winnie. That quality and diligence showed in our relatively new café doing as well as it was. Uncontrollably moaning—again—around the last bite of our new pastry, the Pucker Cream Puff, nicknamed PCP, because it was life-altering, I washed my hands and set myself to doing some actual work.

As I chopped, I attempted to stay on task, but my mind kept wandering. Utterly unacceptable. Uneven fruit bits in the Feisty Fruit Cups would not pass my quality inspection, but despite my best efforts, I continued struggling to stay focused. I kept thinking back to the Goddess card I'd pulled that morning and what it could mean for my day.

I have this ritual, you see. Every morning, while getting ready, I pull a Goddess card for daily spiritual guidance. It's been an important part of my routine for years. The cards never let me down. In fact, I credited them with helping me manifest the café.

That day, six months earlier, Kevin and I had gone to lunch for a preliminary discussion about our mutual dream. On the way back to the car, we'd walked past a storefront with a lease sign. My card from that morning, which had given me the push to jump in, was the Greek goddess Eos. Eos represents new beginnings, lust, and adventure. Since I'd learned to listen to my cards—and so had Kevin—we'd called and started the process to lease, on the spot. A short time later, The Frisky Bean went from dream to reality. And here we were.

That same oh-so-powerful card was the one causing me so much emotional turmoil. Last time, I'd already been thinking about a transition so all I'd felt was excitement. But, getting such a powerful, life-altering card on a random day? I wasn't prepared for any more life-altering. I was still too busy with my previously altered life as it was. In the deep recesses of my mind, a new idea was poking at me, but no way was I ready for *that*. Life was good. I wouldn't want anything to risk destabilizing it. Goosebumps rose on my arms even as butterflies played in my stomach. Was I ready? I really didn't—

"Oh, shit! Motherfucker!"

I booked it to the nearest sink, threw the knife in, and quickly engulfed my finger in cold water.

Kevin rushed over, concern clear on his face and in his tone. "What the hell happened?"

"I won the lottery. What do you think happened? I cut my finger off."

"Don't take that tone with me, you big baby. Now let me see it."

I held out my hand for his inspection as I looked, away sure that part of my finger was going to be dangling there like some mob boss movie. "Is it bad? Am I losing a finger? Dammit! I'm losing a finger, aren't I?"

I felt the eye roll coming off of Kevin's tone. "Hon, you're clearly losing something, but it isn't your finger. It's barely worse than a paper cut. You'll survive."

I dared to look at my mortal wound, and yeah, okay, it wasn't *that* bad. Losing a finger would have definitely been a change, but clearly this wasn't what the goddess's guidance had been referring to. While I stared, transfixed, at the thin line of blood that appeared just at the tip of my index finger on my left hand, Kevin disappeared and reappeared with a Band-Aid from the medical kit in the office. He gently wrapped it around and I watched as my not-so-mortal wound disappeared.

"Wanna tell me why you're so distracted that you're cutting yourself? It isn't like you to be careless or graceless while we bake. Other times, absolutely. But here? No way. You look—" He gave me a once-over. "—anxious."

I considered his question and my answer as he turned away, washed his hands, and wandered back to his own workspace. He continued his earlier preparations, scooping mounds of "Sultry" Snickerdoodles onto a baking sheet because nothing but a lost limb would distract him from a smooth-running kitchen. When it came to baking and business,

Kevin was all schedules, game plans, and potentially baked-goodness-world-domination. Nothing would come between him and our success.

Also, as my childhood best friend, he knew when I needed my space, like right then. So, instead of pressing me for answers he went back to work and waited patiently.

I took the silent space he provided and continued to consider my answer while doing mindless tasks. I washed the knife twice in scorching water and carefully set it aside. Then, I cleaned up the whole station, sanitizing it and tossing potentially contaminated fruit away. Finally, after covering my injured hand with a glove, I kept on working. Seeing as how distraction got me injured in the first place, I wasn't ready to handle the knife just yet, so I grabbed some mandarin oranges, peeled and put a few slices into each cup. A safe part of my routine.

Thoughts collected, I started to explain in a rush of words, "I don't think anxious is quite right, but I'm not sure if I have a better word. I'm feeling... restless? Or maybe uncertain?"

Ugh! This was *sooo* not like me. *Get your shit together and stop being such a Nervous Nellie!* I took a slow, deep, calming breath and tried again.

"It's probably nothing. I'm not sure why I'm so weirded out, but do you remember that Goddess card I got the day we leased this place? Well, I got her today and I guess since I don't feel ready for any major upheavals right now," though my mind briefly alighted on that one new idea I'd been flirting with, "I'm all out of sorts. It's probably nothing."

There. That sounded almost coherent and like I was back to making sense.

I picked up the knife again, ready to tackle the rest of the fruit, when Kevin scolded from across the kitchen, "If you're handling that knife again, you better fucking relax or you'll end up chopping the fruit into varying sizes or actually losing a finger. You know the first shit don't fly and the second will throw my baking schedule off for the whole day and that don't fly either. Anyway, you're probably right."

Kevin smirked while saying this, which had me narrowing my eyes at him. Before I could inquire about that smirk, though, he continued, "Of course, maybe some hot guy will sweep you off your feet today.

That would be a life change you could use. Hell, that would be a life change *I* could use. Could I get that card next?" His smirk turned wicked. "Maybe we could have a good ol' cat fight over today's hot lover?"

"Uh-huh." I gave him my unamused face. Truth was, Kevin was a beautiful Black man. His arm muscles bunched beneath his tight t-shirt as he put the trays in the oven, taking out others that were ready. He looked like the love child of Blair Underwood and the Black Panther himself, Chadwick Boseman. Of medium height, dark, beautiful soulful eyes, and a smile for days. I would never want to compete with him for a man. No way would I win that battle.

Still, what kind of friend would I be if I let him throw down like that without dishing it right back? "You know I'd totally take you in that fight, right? I got my ninja skills on lockdown."

"Girl, you wouldn't even be able to get into a ninja outfit without falling down. I'm not even sure I'd have to fight you. You'd take two steps my way and knock yourself out on a counter."

Warmth suffused me, surely blotching my pale cheeks. Bantering with Kevin was one of my favorite pastimes. I lamented to him, while returning to my chopping, "Damn. It sucks when your friends know walking is your Achilles' heel."

"Tabling the hot men for now—"

"Yes. Tables of hot men. I'll take that, please."

"Quiet down, hussy. As I was saying, all I have left after the cookies, is to cool the 3B and then work on some more muffins and scones. I made extra 3B since we've been running out of it lately. Who knew it would be our best seller? I guess after that *Fifty Shades* book everyone thinks they're into BDSM."

"Oh! That reminds me. I came up with a name for the almond coconut balls we've been planning. What do you think of Sweet Hairy Balls?" I waggled my eyebrows at him.

"I don't think I want to know how you came up with that. Or maybe I do. Either way, it's perfection. Who doesn't like some Sweet Hairy Balls?" He snorted. "I'll add those into the baking rotation starting tomorrow morning. Now back to business, lazy bones."

We settled into a companionable silence working side by side. Our morning prep was like a perfected ballet. All movement efficient, effective, and creating beauty. In our case, edible beauty. Baking was the only place that I ever felt graceful. I was usually tripping over my own feet—and had the bruises to prove it—but when I baked, somehow my mind shut down, the world receded, and I flowed. That was the best way I could describe it, and I craved the high it gave me regularly.

An hour later, I gazed at the tempting tray of completed 3B—or Bondage Banana Bread—our signature baked good. After the bread cooled, I'd sliced it and laid the pieces out in a single layer. Then, I wrapped thin strips of sugared banana around them and brûléed the banana onto the bread. I couldn't help the fact that my mouth watered every single time, and this time had been no different. They could be classified as a dessert, they were so decadently delicious.

I picked up the finished tray and notified Kevin I was going to open. Pushing through the swinging kitchen door with my hip, I set the tray in the display case. With one last review of my comfortably small, beloved café, I made sure everything was ready to go. Warm and inviting as usual. The five rectangle-shaped tables with seating for two were all clean and orderly. In the two far corners, the comfy couches and chairs around low wood and metal tables were also neat and organized. All was in place.

I loved the ambiance we'd created with the warm mustard color we had chosen for the walls and even more so loved the pictures hanging there. They were provided by a local photographer, who preferred to remain anonymous, to showcase their work and sell them.

The images were black and white and suggestive. An obscure body part here, a rounded body part there. I found them evocative, classy, and also sexy as hell. Perfect for our theme and for my inner sex kitten, assuming I actually had one of those that is. I was no novice with my sexuality, but none of the guys I'd dated or slept with so far had ever fully done it for me. Sex was... mmm... okay, but I wanted so much more. I wanted fireworks. Maybe throw in some kink. Something. My toys had more game than the men I'd been dating lately.

In many ways, the theme of the café was my and Kevin's way of sending out into the universe a request for passion, since he felt much the same as I did. I hoped some someones out there were listening.

Maybe the Goddess card was, like Kevin predicted, about a new relationship. Part of me was excited by the prospect and part of me didn't have time for anything else. After having a brief reprieve, finishing up my part of prepping, I was right back to distraction like I'd been earlier. With a wistful sigh, I made my way around the counter of the display case and unlocked the door, flipping the sign to *Open*.

I turned to walk back and, "Dang it!" dropped my keys, because of course I did. In my frustration, I let out a low scream from between my teeth, as the keys loudly clattered to the floor. There was nothing for it. I leaned over to grab them and, of course, that's when I heard the door open behind me. Still bent over, realization that I'd given our first customer of the day quite the backside view struck me much like puberty did... embarrassingly. Mortified, I startled into action. Unfortunately, I swung up too fast and fell backward into whoever had come in. Strong arms wound around me and my breath caught even as my heart raced at the feel of muscles. Lots of yummy muscles and—*oh* my—heat. Heat that radiated from those arms straight into my torso, osmosis style. Somehow, that heat traveled south at warp speed.

"Oh, shit!" The words escaped before I could professionally temper them. So, of course, I stumbled over my words too, "I'm so, so sorry. I... I..." I grudgingly stepped out of the arms and spun. I planned to offer my apologies for the ass view, the falling, and the bad language. I planned to be a good store owner and make it up to whoever was there. I planned, and I failed, because when I got my first sight of the stranger, my jaw dropped low and the only thing that fell out was, "Holy fuck!"

What. The. Hell? Summer!

Yes. That's right. That's what I said. And, clearly following the path paved in regrets I was on, I blushed, my blood rushing through my veins at an all too familiar pace, turning my face warm and blotchy, while a coppery taste entered my mouth. *Fuckity, fuck, fuck!* If I hadn't been wearing clothes, we'd both see the flush covering me, head to toe. Every redhead's bane.

The handsome Norse godlike creature who stood there, amusement clear in his face, had butterflies hitting my stomach in full migration. His absolutely lickable lips curled up on one side, and his eyes were crinkled at the corners. And now that I had licking on the mind, really, his whole body looked as lickable as a giant lollipop of male proportions.

Why was I pooling drool in my mouth instead of forming words? Only the goddess would know, but words continued to fail me. *Those bastards!* I needed some goddamn words. Words that didn't amount to cussing at my customer. I tried, again, to remind myself that I had a business to run, but geez, his way-taller-than-me muscular build—*Was he six feet?*—had shut my brain right down.

So I did the only thing I could do.

Absolutely nothing.

Priceless.

I just stood there gaping. Gaping and watching as his hazel—of course, they had to be hazel—eyes crinkled even more. Since I had nothing better to do with my brain cells in hibernation, I pondered the universe. More specifically why the universe saw fit to throw gods in the way of mere mortals and then, insult to injury, wrap all that perfection in a sexy business suit of dark gray, with a crisp white shirt unbuttoned at his throat. That was just downright mean. I was calling foul!

With my search for words being absolutely useless, I remembered I still had my damn keys to get, so I bent down to grab them because, why not?

His groan above alerted me to my miscalculation. You see, we'd still been standing relatively close together when I reached down. With that brilliant move, I found my head in dangerous proximity to his groin. His now slightly bulging groin. Or was that my imagination?

It took a moment, because it really was a lovely view, but I came back to my senses. I'd been caught ogling his groin. *Yikes!* I averted my eyes and swiftly grabbed for the slippery-as-fuck keys. That's when I heard Kevin, who must have come in from the kitchen, say, "Oh, honey. If you want to do that, you may want to turn that sign back to *Closed*. I don't blame you, though. Welcome to The Frisky Bean. Coffee? Tea? Me? Please tell me it's me."

All I wanted was for the ground to open and swallow me whole. Thinking about opening and swallowing, with my head where it was, proved a really bad idea that left me damp and dying all at once. I finally had the keys in my grasp and somehow made it to a standing position without falling over, and glared at Kevin. Finding my voice—hallelujah—I growled out, "Kevin Dwayne Johnson! That is *not* an appropriate way to greet a customer!"

Of course, neither was yours. Whatever.

I turned toward said customer, only to find him still silently sporting a sexy-as-sin grin. His eyes, though... *Damn*, his eyes held a warm heat I was pretty sure was directed my way, and my insides liquified. I thought I heard Kevin snort and mumble under his breath, "Pot, kettle, black, sister." Then there was silence as the door to the kitchen swooshed and I assumed Kevin left.

"I... am... so... incredibly... sorry... for everything that has happened in the last few minutes. Can we please pretend none of this ever happened? None of it. Ever."

Catch the rest of Summer and Jason's shenanigans in Frisky Intentions found at www.books2read.com/friskyintentions or signed from my website www.michellemars.com. Also, please join my newsletter to keep up with anything new I'm working on at michellemars.com/extras/newsletter/ .

ABOUT THE AUTHOR

For updates go to www.michellemars.com and register to her newsletter.

Michelle Mars has an unhealthy obsession with coffee, caramel, and funny t-shirts. This single mom of two amazing, kind, and creative dragons/children has naturally purple hair and loves nothing more than talking books, kids, and living your best life. She enjoys reading romance, traveling, and writing stories that make her readers laugh, sweat, and swoon.

Author of the steamy, paranormal, sci-fi, rom-com Love Wars Series; Moving Jack, Chasing Rory, and Embracing Irina (A Rosh Hashanah Novella) out now, and Claiming Jill, coming soon.

The first full-length novel in her contemporary rom-com series, The Frisky Bean, Frisky Intentions, is out now and Frisky Business is coming in 2023. She hopes you enjoyed getting a taste of what's to come with this prequel short story, Frisky Connections.

Michelle's truth: Humor is a turn-on!

ALSO BY MICHELLE MARS

Frisky Intentions - Book 1 of The Frisky Bean series.

Other Work:
Moving Jack, Love Wars Book 1

Both covers sold in print and signed by me from my website www.michellemars.com. Illustrated cover available in print, ebook, and audiobook.

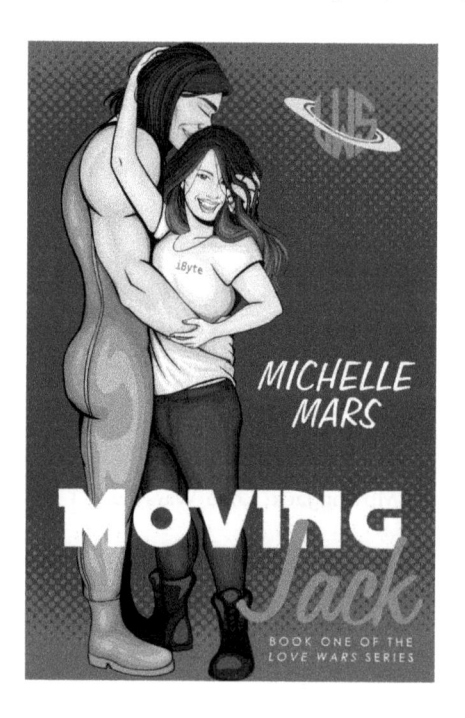

Chasing Rory, Love Wars Book 2

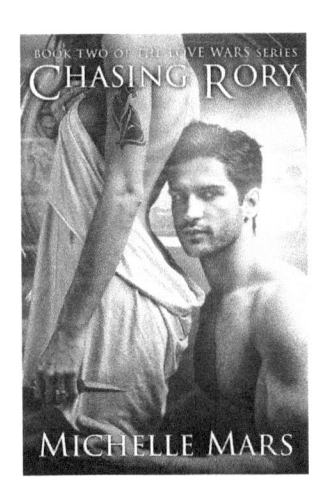

Both covers sold in print and signed by me from my website www.michellemars.com. Illustrated cover available in print, ebook, and audiobook.

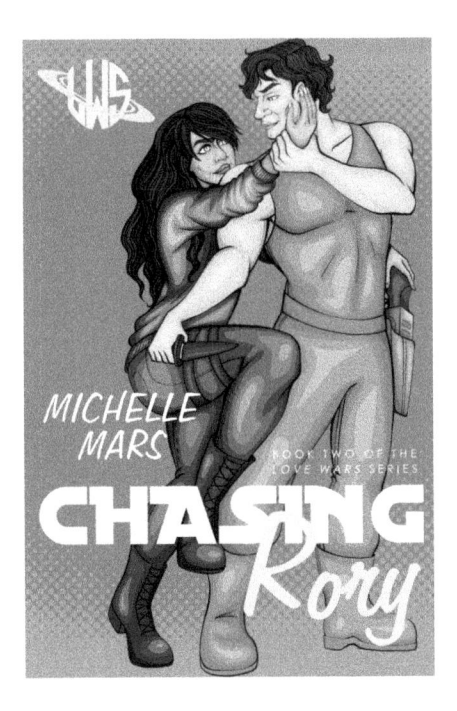

Embracing Irina, Love Wars Book 0.5 Prequel

Both covers sold in print and signed by me from my website www.michellemars.com. Illustrated cover available in print, ebook, and audiobook.

HAPPY ROSH HASHANAH

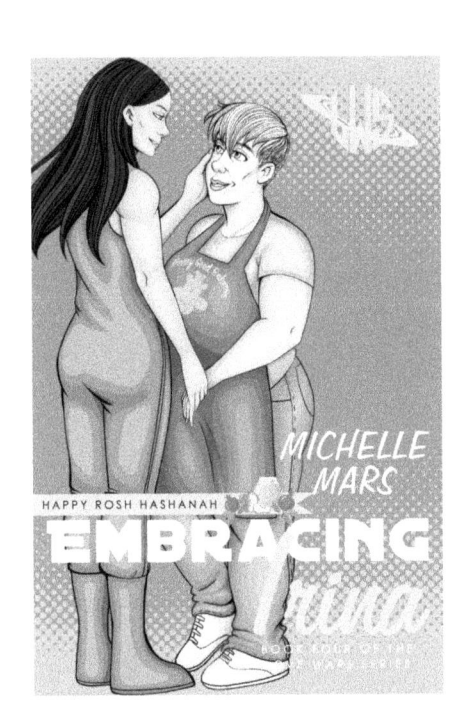

MICHELLE MARS

EMBRACING
Trina

BOOK FOUR OF THE ... SERIES

Milton Keynes UK
Ingram Content Group UK Ltd.
UKHW021330080424
440807UK00008B/712